APRIL PULLEY SAYRE

CITYSCAPE

WHERE SCIENCE AND ART MEET

GREENWILLOW BOOKS

AN IMPRINT OF HarperCollins Publishers

Rectangle.
Right angle.
Window.
Wall.

A windy canyon
where shadows fall.

Lines merge,
diverge, divide.

Science, math, art
live side by side.

Curve

and arch.

Triangle.
Tower.

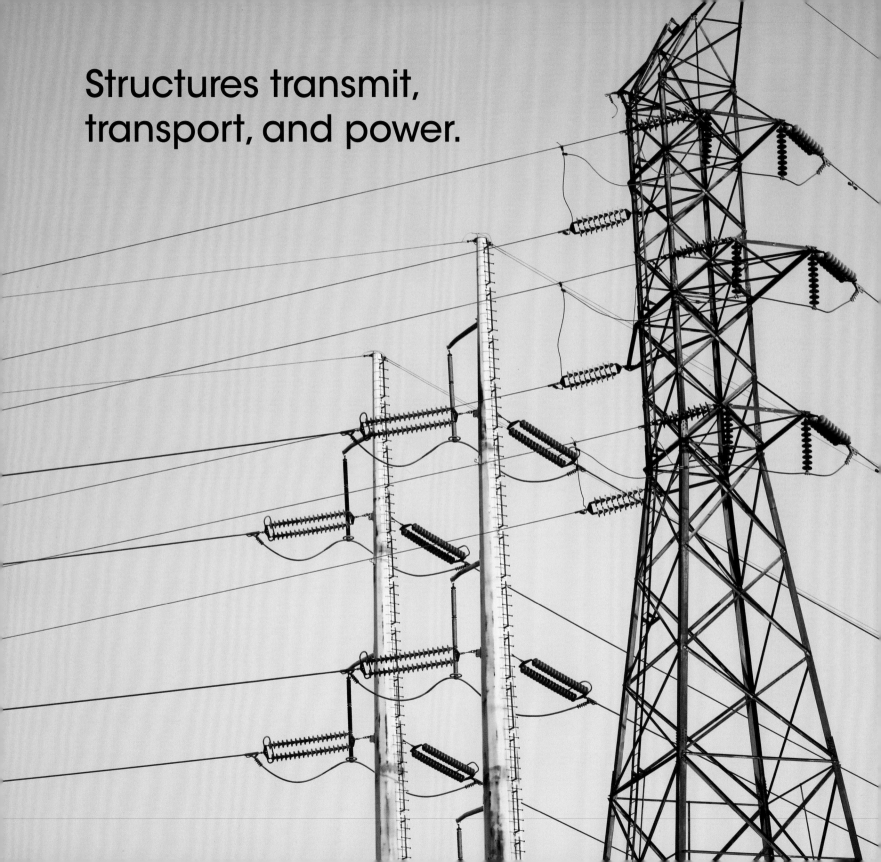

Structures transmit,
transport, and power.

Roofs.

Rows.

Columns.

Ceilings
face
floors.

We enter and exit
wheels and doors.

Bricks
and
blocks—
if they
could talk!

Sea creatures swim—
fossils in rock.

Clouds
paint pictures
as they pass.

Reflections warp
in window glass.

Edges
form
ledges,

lettering,
and
lanes.

Pilings and trusses
bolster bridges
and trains.

Gear teeth mesh.
Axles spin.

COUNTER-
WEIGHT

Pulleys
and levers
haul up
and in.

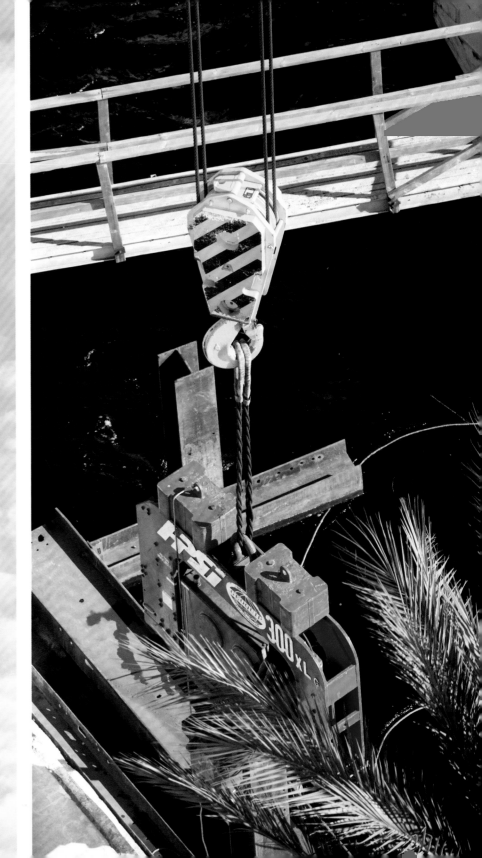

Tension.
Suspension.

Materials. Mass.

Liquids and solids.
Vapors and gas.

Engineers,
artists,
architects

love each line.

Cities shine.

EXPLORE THE CITY

In a city, science, technology, engineering, math, and art are around every corner. Rivers run, canals channel, pistons pump, and buildings rise. Park trees are planted  and traffic flows. Every column, tower, vent, and viewpoint grows from an idea influenced by land, weather, and wind. Architects, stonemasons, carpenters, artists, city planners, plumbers, gardeners, and others dream up, sketch, build, and repair a city's structures. Maybe it seems like a stone building has been there forever—but it has not. Cities change. From green roofs to gables, from sidewalks to spires, someone's ideas will shape the city of the future. Will they be yours?

 Take a look at a city. If you can, wander and wonder. Perhaps photograph, sketch, measure, and study the cityscape. As you dig in, sort through the questions on these pages and see which make you curious, and where they lead. Add your own observations and questions. Asking questions leads to new systems to support city life. Those ideas may sprout in your notebook or your neighborhood or perhaps in a city far away, across the earth. Innovation sprouts from cities, old and new, large and small. City ideas can cross-pollinate, giving a better future for city dwellers everywhere.

Questions to Ponder As You Wander

❋ Trees can transport water from the soil to their top leaves. How do people get water up to the top of a skyscraper?
❋ What kinds of columns are there, and what do they do?
❋ Buildings weigh a lot. How do people prevent them from sinking into the ground?
❋ What do all those vents and ducts on the outsides of buildings do?
❋ What kinds of systems help people move through cities?
❋ Why are towers shaped the way they are?
❋ How are skyscrapers built?
❋ Why are some tall buildings made to shift in the wind, and how do people minimize movement in others?

How do people earthquake-proof buildings?

Where does drinking water come from in the city?

Who plans the parks?

How do people protect buildings from lightning?

Where does city food come from?

What are green rooftops, and why are people building them?

What is a heat island?

Who decides when the lights turn red, yellow, or green?

Why are so many cities built along rivers and shores?

Where does all the waste go?

How do they clean the windows on skyscrapers?

Why do people build arches?

How does a revolving door work?

Why are city streets windy sometimes?

Where does rain from a storm go in a city?

How are cities adapting to climate change?

How old are the buildings in cities?

Do city planners think about sounds?

Where do pigeons nest?

How do animals other than people survive in the city?

How do people plan and paint the big murals?

Who creates sculptures in parks?

Can buildings be art?

How do suspension bridges stay up?

How do people construct bridges across waterways without falling in?

Why is there a rush hour, and what do people do to make it better?

How is concrete made, and why does it need to cool?

What kinds of things are transported through a city?

What are the oldest cities on Earth?

Who helps architects figure out how to build a building?

Who maps out city streets and which way they run?

Who is going to plan how a city will work in the future?

Library of Congress Cataloging-in-Publication Data
Names: Sayre, April Pulley, author. Title: Cityscape : where science and art meet / by April Pulley Sayre.
Description: First edition. | New York, NY : Greenwillow Books, an Imprint of HarperCollins Publishers, (2020)
   | Audience: Ages 4–8. | Audience: Grades K–1. | Summary: Photographs and easy-to-read, rhyming
   text introduce how basic STEAM concepts can be found in the architecture, building, construction,
   and transportation of city life. Includes notes about what to look for while wandering through a city.
Identifiers: LCCN 2019041786 | ISBN 9780062893314 (hardcover)
Subjects: CYAC: City and town life—Fiction.
Classification: LCC PZ8.3.S2737 Cit 2020 | DDC (E)—dc23
LC record available at https://lccn.loc.gov/2019041786

20 21 22 23 24 ROT 10 9 8 7 6 5 4 3 2 1 First Edition   Greenwillow Books

For the dreamers
and the builders
—A. P .S.

ACKNOWLEDGMENTS

Thank you to my family: to Lyd, the adventure wizard; to Cat, my
city guide; to photo adventurers Rodney, Nora, Winston, and Turner.
Thank you, also, to Karen Romano Young, Karyn Lewis Bonfiglio,
and Lyn and Jay Ferriero.

PHOTOGRAPHS ● FRONT COVER

Optima Signature building, Chicago, Illinois, architect David C.
Hovey. Photo by April Pulley Sayre, 2019

PHOTOGRAPHS ● BACK COVER

Jay Pritzker Pavilion, Millennium Park, Chicago, architect Frank
Gehry. Photo by April Pulley Sayre, 2018

PHOTOGRAPHS ● INTERIOR

1: Reflection of buildings in *Cloud Gate*, sculpture by artist Sir Anish
Kapoor, Millennium Park, Chicago. 2–3: JW Marriott, Indianapolis,
Indiana; sunrise over Lake Michigan reflected in windows of 875
North Michigan Avenue, Chicago; window in adobe wall, Phoenix,
Arizona. 4–5: Buildings, Chicago River, and Lake Michigan,
Chicago; the Rink at Rockefeller Center, New York City, New York
(photo by Nora Willett); The Willard Hotel, Washington, DC. 6–7:
Metro Center Station, Washington, D.C.; *Lions*, sculpture by Edward
and Laura Kemeys, Art Institute of Chicago; bench detail, South
Bend, Indiana; building detail, Washington, DC. 8–9: Curved
window and bougainvillea, Phoenix, Arizona; arch, Chicago;
Jay Pritzker Pavilion, Chicago. 10–11: Tower in Chicago; tower in
Miami (photo by Rodney Willett); tower in London, England (photo
by Rodney Willett); flowers in Lurie Garden, Chicago. 12–13: High-
tension power lines, Gary, Indiana; scooters, Hanoi, Vietnam
(photo by Rodney Willett); fire station, Chicago; kayak, Chicago;
school bus and United States Capitol, Washington, DC. 14–15:
Rooftops in Prague, Czech Republic (photo by Nora Willett); rows
and columns of panels on Hilton Garden Inn Downtown Riverwalk,
Chicago, architects David Ervin and Ryan von Drehle; Marina
City, Chicago, architect Bertrand Goldberg; Thomas Jefferson
Memorial, Washington, DC. 16–17: Sagrada Família,
Barcelona, Spain, architect Antoni Gaudí (photo
by Rodney Willett); mosaic floor, Ostia Antica,
Italy (photo by Nora Willett); Centennial
Wheel, Chicago; Angkor Wat, Cambodia
(photo by Turner Willett); revolving door, Washington, DC. 18–
19: Machu Picchu, Peru (photo by Rodney Willett); brick detail
from *City of Altruism*, mural by Gaia, Greenville, South Carolina;
ammonite fossils, Pittsfield Building, Chicago. 20–21: Clouds and
buildings, Chicago; buildings, Phoenix. 22–23: Optima Sonoran
Village, Scottsdale, Arizona; rock dove, Washington, DC; Main
Street Bridge, Jacksonville, Florida. 24–25: Drawbridge, Florida;
Wells Street Bridge, Chicago; Main Street Bridge, Jacksonville.
26–27: Bridge gears, Chicago; construction crane, New York
City; lowering pilings into riverfront, Jacksonville. 28–29: Sunshine
Skyway Bridge, St. Petersburg, Florida; Talmadge Memorial Bridge,
Savannah, Georgia. 30–31: Frost on tire tread, South Bend, Indiana;
industrial scene, Houston, Texas; street repairs, Washington, DC;
fountain with flowers in background, Chicago. 32–33: The Louvre
Pyramid, Paris, France, architect I.M. Pei (photo by Rodney
Willett); fountain, Detroit Metropolitan Airport, Detroit, Michigan.
34–35: Fountain tiles, Phoenix; roof truss detail, Washington, D.C.;
gargoyle, Chicago; Aqua, Chicago, architect Jeanne Gang.
36–37: Tower Bridge, London (photo by Rodney Willett); DuSable
Bridge and Chicago River, Chicago; Earth by Leonello Calvetti/
Science Photo Library. 38–39: People waiting for bats to emerge
from under the Anne W. Richards Congress Avenue Bridge, Austin,
Texas. Insets: Art Institute of Chicago; Machu Picchu, Peru; fountain
detail, Greenville, South Carolina; fountain, Houston, Texas; tower,
New York City; window washers, Indianapolis; market stall food,
Hanoi; starling, Washington, DC; drawbridge, Lake Shore Drive,
Chicago; highway, Chicago; coneflowers, Lurie Garden, Chicago.
40: Grackle near adobe and fruit tree, Scottsdale, Arizona.